This Book Belongs to

A Christmas Secret

A story by
Candace Hall

Publishing assistance by KJ Waters Consultancy
www.kjwconsultancy.com.

Dedication

Dedicated to my mother, Dixie Irvin, who rescued

O'Malley when he was abandoned as a kitten. His real

life story inspired this book.

NOW DASH AWAY ALL

The air was crisp and cold, snowflakes swirling everywhere. The reindeer were restless knowing Christmas Eve was soon to arrive.

Prancer nudged Comet and said, "It's finally time."

Comet yawned and answered, "Christmas comes but once a year."

All of Santa's reindeer began prancing and snorting in anticipation. Over in the dark corner, the hay rustled and a pair of antlers began to appear from within the haystack. Ever so slowly at first, then with a sudden rush and flutter, a reindeer head suddenly appeared.

"What's all the commotion about?" Dasher asked.

"It's Christmas Eve!" answered Prancer. "It's time, everyone; It's time!"

The ruckus the reindeer made could be heard all throughout the North Pole.

Elves began scurrying even faster than before.

"Hurry! We must get the sleigh ready."

Broome was Santa's chief elf. Broome knew what had to be done and would oversee the young elves as preparations began. Elves danced around a shiny red sleigh as the reindeer were harnessed with bells for the flight.

The toys were wrapped with bright ribbons and bows. Broome climbed aboard the sleigh.

The elves all shouted, "It's time now, Santa! Up and Away!"

The moon was full and the stars were bright. With a crack of the whip, Santa's voice rang out, "On Donner, on Cupid, Dasher, Dancer, Prancer, Comet, Vixen and Blitzen."

Pulling the sleigh with all of their might, the team sprang into the night. The trip bringing toys to all the good boys and girls around the world began.

A REINDEER SURPRISE

The sleigh settled gently on the snow covered roof. In the twinkle of an eye, Santa and his bag of toys vanished down the chimney. The harness bells jingled as the reindeer shook with delight.

Above the reindeer's breath a small cry could be heard. Dasher leaned forward and stared at the snow.

"Did you hear that?"

Prancer turned his head in the direction where the sound was last heard. Again came the faintest of cries.

"It's here," Cupid said. "Quick! Look over here!"

Far below, amidst all the snow, was a tiny black figure. Try as it might, it could not move through the snow. The faint cry drifted upward toward the reindeer.

Broome stood up in the sleigh and bellowed at Dasher, "Hurry! Get down and see what's in the snow."

Dasher, straining and pulling at the harness, finally slipped free and leapt from the rooftop to the shadow below.

"Hmmm," said Dasher as he walked around the snow.

Finally sticking his nose low, he heard a hissing sound and got a scratch on the nose. Quickly pulling his head up, he cried, "It's a cat! And he scratched me."

The reindeer all began laughing at Dasher.

Broome yelled down, "Find his home and let it be done. Santa will soon return."

Dasher looked left, then he looked right, but nowhere did he find other prints in the snow.

"I can't find his home," Dasher replied.

The kitten now lay still in the snow. Dasher gently nudged the tiny black cat.

The kitten tried to raise his head, his eyes blinked at Dasher, as he whispered, "Please help me."

The reindeer looked sadly at one another and agreed, "We can't leave him here; he'll not survive."

"I know," Dasher said, "Let's put him in the hay sack; that will warm him up."

"Be careful with him Dasher," Broome

cautioned.

Flying swiftly, Dasher held the kitten in his mouth ever so tenderly and nestled him down in the bag.

The kitten shivered as he tried to snuggle into the hay. In a trembling voice the kitten cried "I am so very cold."

Dasher began to nuzzle the hay warming the kitten.

Reaching up with his tiny paw, the kitten touched Dasher's nose and asked "Are you my family?"

Dasher looked at Broome and asked, "What shall we do?"

Broome reminded Dasher that only those born in the North Pole have a home there. "It's the magic, remember?"

Dasher rushed back to the ground, hoping to find one trace of the kitten's home. The kitten's prints stopped at a mailbox marked O'Malley. The house was empty and bare. Broome waved for Dasher to return.

With a burst of laughter and a rush of air, Santa jumped from the chimney back to the sleigh. The reindeer all giggled and got into place, so happy their secret was safe.

"Back to work we go," Santa yelled and pulled on the reins.

As the reindeer leapt from the rooftop, Broome looked back and saw the name O'Malley on the mailbox.

Glancing at the sack of hay, Broome sighed, "O'Malley is a good name."

HEAR THE MOUSE ROAR

"What a wonderful night!" Santa shouted as the sleigh slipped into the barn at the North Pole. "Berries and hay for my reindeer, cookies and hot cocoa for Broome and me," Santa said patting his belly.

"What now?" Dasher asked as Santa and Broome left the barn.

Rocking back and forth, the bag of hay spilled over and out tumbled a very sleepy kitten. Staring up at Dasher, O'Malley began to cry in the most pitiful way.

The reindeer began talking amongst themselves saying, "He's hungry. How shall we feed him?" They all looked at the floor in dismay.

The hay around O'Malley began to move, and a little nose surrounded by whiskers appeared. It was a mouse. The mouse carefully sniffed at the kitten.

O'Malley shivered and cried again. The mouse moved closer. Dasher stamped his hoof at the mouse to scare it off. The mouse looked up at Dasher and showed her most ferocious look.

Standing on its hind legs the mouse yelled, "I am Wilma, mother of four, let not this monster hurt my young!"

Dasher lowered his head toward O'Malley and said, "He is an orphan and starving; he cannot hurt anyone."

Wilma crept close to O'Malley. The kitten tried to open his eyes, but his head fell back onto the hay.

Wilma reached out and patted O'Malley on the nose. "We must hurry," Wilma cried as she scurried back to her home. Gathering her family, they raced through the snow to Santa's house. Quietly slipping under the door, they made their way to the kitchen where Mrs. Claus was heating milk for hot cocoa.

Wilma decided she would distract Mrs. Claus while the rest of the family would get some milk for O'Malley. Wilma jumped up onto the countertop doing somersaults and cartwheels, knocking over anything in her way.

Mrs. Claus began to laugh and follow after Wilma as she continued her antics. Milk went splashing along the countertop then onto the floor into a small bowl the mice had placed there.

Carefully, they pushed the bowl back to the barn where they placed it under O'Malley's nose. Wilma dipped her paw in the milk and wiped it on O'Malley's lips. O'Malley did not move.

One by one, Wilma's family began to dip their paws in the milk feeding him one drop at a time. O'Malley's tongue began to lap at the milk as the mice danced with delight.

O'Malley purred loudly at his newfound friends. Content and full, O'Malley licked each mouse and curled up to sleep.

The reindeer received the news of O'Malley's recovery and began to prance and snort about the barn. Soon stories spread throughout the North Pole of its newest addition, a cat, who was not born in the North Pole.

Wilma and her family suddenly faced a new dilemma. O'Malley did not fit in their tiny home.

Wilma asked Dasher, "Does Santa know about O'Malley?"

Dasher and the other reindeer held their heads low and looked at each other ashamed.

"No," answered Dasher. "We just wanted to help save O'Malley; we never thought about where he would live."

"Someone get Broome," Wilma said. "Surely he can help us decide what to do."

Dasher called the elves and mice together for a meeting with Broome. Suddenly the barn door burst open.

"What's wrong?" Broome asked.

The elves fell silent. Broome stared at the elves, reindeer, and mice gathered before him.

Finally, Wilma cleared her throat and said, "Broome, we need to find a home for O'Malley.

Broome said in a sad voice, "Remember only those born in the North Pole can live here; it's the Christmas magic."

"Where is O'Malley?" Dasher asked. Everyone turned to the haystack where O'Malley had been, but alas he was no longer there.

"We must find him!" Wilma cried. Reindeer, mice, and elves scurried about the North Pole to find O'Malley.

THE GREAT ESCAPE

O'Malley had heard what Broome said and decided it was better for him to go. After all, they had saved his life and he did not want to cause any trouble. O'Malley decided to leave the North Pole.

The lights of the North Pole grew dimmer as O'Malley walked in the dark.

The snow began falling heavier, and the icy cold wind slowed his every step. Exhausted, O'Malley curled up beside a snow drift and began to cry, "Where do I belong? I have no home, no family."

Suddenly a huge, warm hand plucked him from the snow and nestled him inside a warm coat.

Everyone in the North Pole searched and searched for O'Malley. After looking everywhere, they all returned to the barn.

Broome, with his head hung low said, "We must tell Santa what we have done, O'Malley is lost."

As they stood on Santa's doorstep, Dasher looked in the window. There sat Santa leaning back in his chair dozing by the fire. Broome knocked gently on the door.

Santa's jolly voice rang out, "Come in, come in."

They all walked silently into the room, dreading telling Santa the news. Suddenly a crash sounded in the corner by Santa's Christmas tree. A shiny ornament slowly rolled across the floor followed by a small black figure. Santa laughed and looked down at O'Malley. Everyone held their breath as they watched O'Malley gently climb onto Santa's lap and curl up in a ball.

Smiling at O'Malley Santa said, "I was wondering when they would tell me about you. The magic of Christmas is love." Santa held O'Malley close to his heart and said, "You are home. Welcome to your new family."

LET'S COUNT

O'Malley found a new home with Santa and Mrs. Claus. Can you help him find the words in red in the illustrations?

Page 4 ~ How many jingle bells can you see in the sleigh?

Page 7 ~ Can you count the number of animal eyes that are showing?

Page 11 ~ O'Malley left some footprints in the snow. How many did you see?

Page 13 ~ The reindeer has jingle bells on his harness. How many can you count?

Page 17 ~ How many animals are in the picture?

Page 19 ~ As Wilma does a cartwheel for Mrs. Claus, how many baby mice are catching the milk below?

Page 23 ~ The reindeer are listening closely to Broome. How many antlers can you count? Do you see O'Malley in the picture?

Page 30 ~ Count the jolly elves surrounding Santa and O'Malley.

Bonus: How many different pictures of O'Malley can you find?

ANSWER KEY

Page 4 ~ There are 9 jingle bells.

Page 7 ~ You can see 17 animal eyes.

Page 11 ~ There are 14 footprints in the snow.

Page 13 ~ The reindeer has 13 jingle bells on his harness.

Page 17 ~ You can find 4 animals in the picture.

Page 19 ~ Four baby mice are catching the milk for O'Malley.

Page 23 ~ The reindeer have 8 antlers, two on each one.

Page 30 ~ Santa and O'Malley are surrounded by 5 jolly elves.

Bonus: O'Malley is in 8 pictures in the book.

CPSIA information can be obtained
at www.ICGtesting.com
Printed in the USA
LVHW020931191120
672147LV00009B/172